It's Great to Skate!

An Easy Guide to In-line Skating

written by
Alexa Witt

illustrated by
Nate Evans

Ready-to-Read
Aladdin Paperbacks

First Aladdin Paperbacks edition May 2000
Also available in a Simon & Schuster Book for Young Readers hardcover edition

Text copyright © 2000 by Alexa Witt
Ilustrations © 2000 by Nate Evans

Aladdin Paperbacks
An Imprint of Simon & Schuster Children's Publishing Division
1230 Avenue of the Americas
New York, NY 10020

All rights reserved, including the right of reproduction
in whole or in part in any form.

READY-TO-READ is a registered trademark of Simon & Schuster, Inc.
The text for this book was set in Utopia.
The illustrations were rendered in watercolor and colored pencil
Printed and bound in the United States of America
2   4   6   8   10   9   7   5   3   1

The Library of Congress has cataloged the hardcover edition as follows:
Witt, Alexa.
It's great to skate! : an easy guide to in-line skating / written by Alexa Witt;
illustrated by Nate Evans.
p.   cm. (Ready-to-Read)
Summary: Offers simple instructions for children learning to use in-line skates.
ISBN 0-689-83109-9 (hc)
1. In-line skating—Juvenile literature. [1. In-line skating—Juvenile]
I. Evans, Nate, ill. II. Title III. Series
GV859.73.W58   2000
796.21—dc21
99-45861
CIP
AC
ISBN 0-689-82590-0 (Aladdin pbk.)

Imagine . . .
you have wheels
instead of feet!

Imagine . . .
you have a pair
of in-line skates!
Now you can go . . . oops!

First you need to learn
how to use your skates.
This book will show you how!

Yes!

First, ask your
Mom or Dad or
the adult in charge,
"Is it okay?"

HURRAY!

No hills.
No cars.

Looks all clear!

Pick a place that has NO hills.
Pick a place that has NO cars.
Pick a place with lots of space:
an empty parking lot,
the playground or the park.
If it's got a smooth blacktop,
it's the perfect place to skate.

Put your helmet on your head.

Pull your elbow pads
over your elbows.

Pull your wrist guards
over your wrists.

Pull your knee pads over your knees.

Put on your thick socks.

Finally, put your feet
into your in-line skates!

Fasten your feet belts.

Tie the laces, buckle the buckles . . .

Make sure your feet are snug.

NOW IT'S TIME TO GO!

Almost.

The first thing you need to know
before you go,
is how NOT to go.

BALANCING

You must learn to stand
without falling down,
or falling over,

or falling back.
Falling is no fun!
But it may happen a lot
because your feet are wheels now,
and wheels roll.

If you roll, you can fall.
If you skate, you can fall.

That is why you wear
knee pads, elbow pads,
wrist guards, and a helmet—
to protect your body
in case you fall.

So hold on, skater!
And get ready.

You are in charge of your feet.
You are in charge of your hips.
You are in charge of your knees.

Bend your knees—
a little, not a lot!
This helps keep
your top part—head, shoulders, and arms—
balancing on
your bottom part—legs, knees, and feet.

Let go!

When you can stand still
without falling down,
or falling over,
or falling back . . .
you are balancing!

Balance is the secret to in-line skating.
It gets easier with practice.

Keep trying!
Keep trying!
Keep trying!

Just one more thing
before you go . . .

HOW TO STOP
On the back
of the in-line skate
on your right foot
is a black, rubber brake.

Inside that skate,
point your toes up.
Push your heel down
into the ground.

When you tilt
your foot back,
the rubber brake
rubs the ground.
Soon you will stop.

Rubber Brake

14

Look ahead of you.
Leave a lot of space
before you stop
in front of a tree—
or the tree may stop you!

Bend those knees!
It helps you brake!

Keep trying!
Keep trying!
Keep trying!

HOW TO GO
That's how to stop.
NOW it's time to go!

Stand on a place that's flat.
Put one foot forward,
bend that knee,
and push off with your back foot!

Glide forward!

Put the other foot forward,
push off with your back foot,
and glide forward!

Put one foot forward,
push off with the other.

Keep going!
Keep going!
Keep going!

When you are going fast,
in-line skating is like
walking in very
slow
motion.

One step, glide.
One step, glide.
One step, glide.

Look Out!

Always look out!

Look for things
that might make you fall.
Then move out of the way,
or use your brake.

See the ball—
Look Out!

See the girl—
Look Out!

See the dog—
Look Out!

If you can't move
out of the way
in time,
shout, "Look out! Look out!"

19

GOING

You can really do it!
You are really rolling!
You are really skating!

The wind is rushing
past your face!
You can move
from place to place.

Skate up the smoothest path!

Glide by the slide.

Balance at the ice cream stand!

Brake by the lake.

Keep up with the dog and cat!
Roll faster than the ball.

Keep your head up so
you do not crash into the wall.

25

Try going up a hill!
Try going to the store!

STORE

OPEN

Why wait and pay
to take a bus?
It's free and fun
to move like us.

So when an adult says, "No more!"
it's time to stop.

It's time to sit.
It's time to take off
your in-line skates, helmet,
wrist guards, elbow pads,
and knee pads.

See what you did today?
Imagine what you will do
the next time
you go in-line skating!